MIDLOTHIAN PUBLIC LIBRARY

3 1614 00099 8253

W9-AGG-848

MIDLOTHIAN
PUBLIC LIBRARY

Midlothian
Public Library

14701 S. Kenton Ave.
Midlothian, IL 60445

DEMCO

...AL PUBLIC LIBRARY
1701 S. KENTON AVE.
MIDLOTHIAN, IL 60445

To My daddy, Dave—in hope

–K.G.B.

I thank God.

I dedicate these illustrations to my grandfather, William H. Thomas, who taught

me to know God, work hard, and to give my best at whatever I'm pursuing.

To my valentine, Tamera Diggs-Tate: I love you.

–D.T.

The Legend of the
VALENTINE

Written by
Katherine Grace Bond

Illustrated by
Don Tate

Zonderkidz

Daddy was in jail. It was all Marcus could think about. Daddy was in jail, and he hadn't done anything bad.

At the next desk, Davey was coloring hearts orangey-red like his hair. He'd drawn fourteen and crossed out five. "I'm counting down to Valentine's," he told Marcus. "Can I borrow a skin-color crayon?"

Marcus ran his finger over his crayons, wondering which one Davey wanted. He handed over a pinkish one, then pulled out a brown for himself.

"That's the wrong color." It was Travis. Marcus kept coloring. Behind him, Travis spoke louder. "Everyone knows that's the wrong color for skin." He laughed as if it were funny.

Marcus kept his eyes on his paper. "There's no wrong color for skin," he said. But he said it quietly so no one would hear.

It had been five months since he'd started at the new school. Mama had said it would be hard. Daddy too. It used to be against the law in Alabama for Marcus to go to a white school. Even when the law changed, not many had tried. But Marcus had wanted to.

Granny had been on his side. "Let the boy go," she'd said. "He's strong. And doesn't he have a band of angels watching over him?"

Some days Marcus looked around the classroom for his band of angels, but in five months he hadn't seen any.

Sometimes singing in church sounded like a band of angels. Lately Daddy had been driving all the way from Hope to the big church in Selma to hear Dr. Martin Luther King.

But now Daddy was in jail and Dr. King was too.

Marcus colored himself into his picture, behind gray bars.

At lunchtime, Davey was sitting alone like Marcus usually did. Marcus sat down, and Davey didn't move away.

"Hey, Brown-Crayon!" Marcus didn't have to turn around to know it was Travis. Jack and Bern were with him.

"Hear your daddy's in jail," Travis said. Jack and Bern giggled. Travis gave Davey's orange hair a tug. "Kumquat head!" he said. "Why are you eating lunch with the jail boy?"

Davey blushed.

Travis flipped Marcus's plate. Mashed potatoes and gravy splatted into his lap. "Oops!" called Travis, as he and Jack and Bern ran out the door.

Davey waited until they were gone. He handed Marcus some napkins. "Don't feel bad," he said. "Travis did the same things to me before you came."

Marcus cleaned the gravy off his good school pants. He couldn't look at Davey.

Granny was hanging up her hat when Marcus got home. "Did you try and register again?" he asked her. "Did they let you?"

In the kitchen, Mama shook her head. Every week Granny tried to register to vote. Every week they told her the registrar's office was closed. That was why Daddy and Dr. King and a lot of other people were in jail down in Selma. They wanted everyone to be able to vote.

Granny set a stack of library books on the reading shelf. "How was school?" she asked.

"Fine," Marcus said. "It was just fine." Granny peered at him as if she were checking his temperature. If she asked too many questions, Marcus would get her to tell him a story. Granny knew stories about everything. Mama set down some gingersnaps and a glass of milk.

Almost Valentine's Day," Granny said. "Best get started on those cards." She plunked down scissors and paste and a box of saved wrapping paper from Christmas. "There's enough to make real nice ones for everyone."

Marcus looked away from her. His stomach hurt. "Don't feel like it," he said in a low voice. Granny didn't answer.

Marcus scuffed his shoes under the table. He thought about Daddy in jail... and mean jailers he'd seen on the news. He thought about Travis, and his stomach hurt worse. Granny waited.

I hate them." The words were like a steel gate swinging open. Other words tumbled out before Marcus could stop them. Words about eating alone and Travis and kids who tripped him in the halls.

Mama held a cupboard door, her jaw set.

"I hate those school kids!" The words felt like fire. "And I hate Travis most of all!"

Granny turned Marcus's face to hers. "No," she said. "No need to be hating. Jesus says to love our enemies."

Mama slammed the cupboard door. "He's just a child!" she said.

Granny laid a hand on her arm. "So's this other boy," she said. "Just a child. They're all children. God's children."

Mama took a breath and let it out. Marcus wondered if there were any angels for Mama.

Granny folded some red paper. "Reminds me of the first Valentine."

Marcus spun the tape with his finger. "What about it?"

"Not it," said Granny. "Him. Valentine was a Christian back when it was against the Roman law."

"Against the law?"

"Oh, yes." Granny cut a curve on the fold. "There was a law that everyone had to worship the emperor. Christians worshiped only Jesus. That seemed strange to the people in Rome. And any time something went wrong back then, folks needed someone to blame."

Mama swept the forks into the sink with a clatter.

Marcus stopped spinning the tape. "So what about Valentine?"

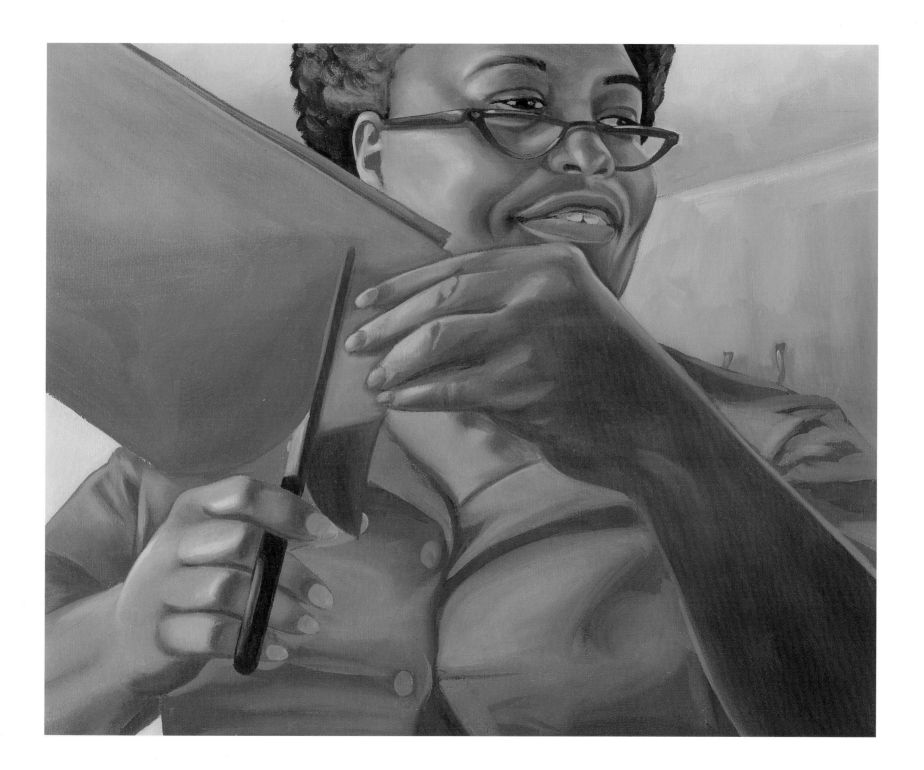

The emperor had Valentine beaten with sticks because he wouldn't worship the emperor."

"Did Valentine fight back?"

"No," said Granny. "That's not the way of Jesus."

On the news, Marcus had seen protestors being beaten with sticks. They hadn't fought back either. *I'd fight back*, thought Marcus.

Granny pulled the cut part out of her paper, leaving a heart-shaped hole.

"So Valentine was thrown in jail," she said.

"Jail!" Marcus sat up. "He didn't do anything bad!"

"That's right," said Granny. "He didn't."

Mama stood at the sink with her back to Granny. Marcus knew she was listening. "Go on," he said.

Well," said Granny, "Valentine's jailer was called Asterius. He worshiped the emperor like everyone else. But Valentine wouldn't stop talking to him about Jesus."

"But that was the jailer!" said Marcus. "He talked to the jailer about that?"

"'Course he did," said Granny. "He sang about Jesus; he prayed to Jesus. Asterius started to get interested." Granny closed her eyes. "Now Asterius had a blind daughter. 'If your Jesus can heal my little girl,' said Asterius, 'then I'll believe in him.'"

"And did he?"

Granny opened her eyes. "'Course he did," she said. "Valentine prayed. The child got her sight. And Asterius was so happy that he and his whole family became Christians."

Marcus fiddled with the paper. He wanted to be happy for the jailer, but he wasn't. Mama went to get the mail. Marcus crumpled Granny's valentine scraps into little red balls.

When she came back, Mama held a letter torn into the shape of a heart.

"From Daddy," she said and kissed the top of Marcus's head.

"Here is my valentine to you all," Mama read. "We're singing in the jail! Some of the jailers are starting to sing along. Sounds like a band of angels. I love you. Have courage. God shall overcome. Daddy."

"Yes," Mama whispered.

Marcus touched the letter's torn edge. Daddy was brave. Marcus didn't feel brave at all. He took a sheet of colored paper. He knew what he had to do.

Valentine's Day. Marcus's stomach hurt as he pulled the big envelope out of his satchel. The teacher had gone to get juice, but she said they could start the party without her.

Carefully, Marcus slid a card into each valentine folder. The last one was the fanciest with ribbon and lace and three kinds of colored paper. He'd spent a long time making it. He took a breath and put it in Travis's folder before Travis could see him. Then he waited in the reading corner.

Travis smiled when he got to Marcus's valentine. Then he scowled as he read the crayoned words: "Let's be friends. From Marcus."

Marcus's stomach clenched, but he didn't hide.

"Someone playing a joke on me?" Travis demanded. "Who did this?"

Everyone stopped. Marcus stepped forward. "I did," he said and looked right at Travis's face.

Don't want to be friends," Travis muttered. He tore the valentine and dropped it as if it had burned him. Everyone was quiet. Marcus didn't let himself look away. He didn't let himself look at his torn valentine.

"Love your enemies," Granny had said. That's what Daddy had done in the jail. That's what Valentine had done all those years ago. Love. Even when some folks didn't deserve it. It was what Jesus wanted him to do.

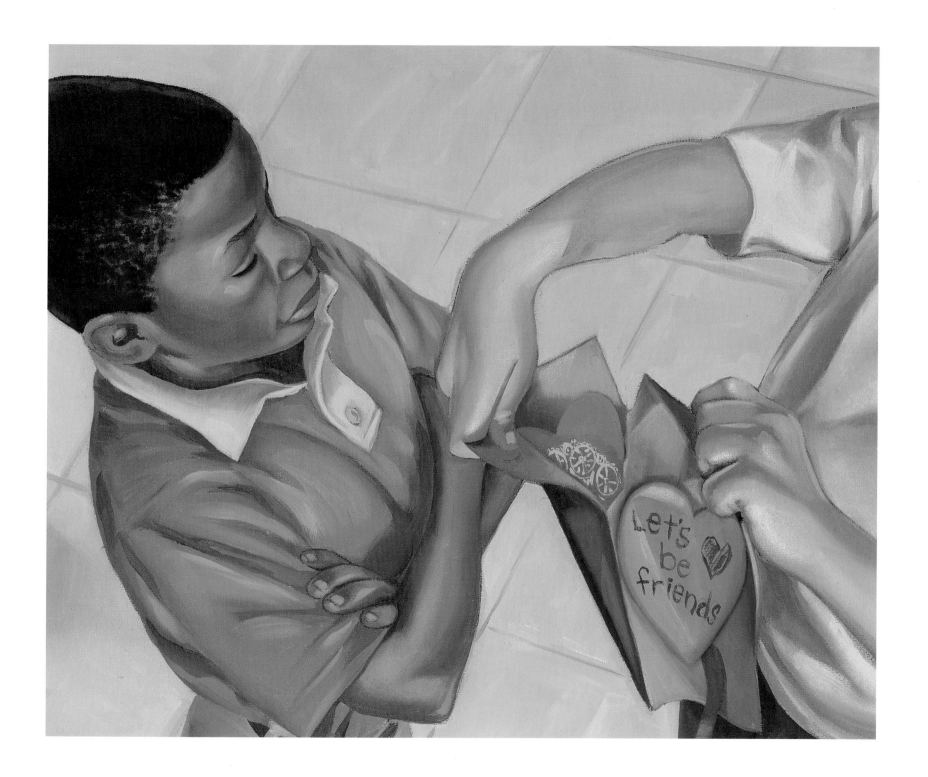

Hey!" It was Davey. Pinned to his shirt was Marcus's valentine. "I want to be friends, Marcus."

"Me, too." Kathy found her valentine from Marcus and pinned it on her dress.

"So do I. I want to be friends." Andy and Margie pinned on Marcus's valentines. Sarah and Tom did too. Even Jack and Bern pinned them on. Slowly, everyone moved forward until Marcus was surrounded. Only Travis sat at his desk, blinking hard as if something was in his eye.

Marcus stepped to the edge of the circle. "Hey," he said softly. "No need to be hating anymore. Come on, Travis." He held out his hand. "Come on."

The History of Saint Valentine

Many different stories are told about a Christian named Valentine who lived **270** years after Jesus. In one, he was a priest in Rome who performed secret marriages after the emperor had forbidden soldiers to marry. In another, he helped Christians who were in prison for their faith. In the most well-known story, he was thrown into prison for worshiping only Jesus and healed the jailer's blind, adopted daughter. When the jailer and his family became Christians, the emperor, "Claudius the Cruel," was so angry he had Valentine killed.

The Civil Rights Movement

Voting was only one right families like Marcus's fought for during the fifties and sixties. In some parts of America, African-Americans and other people of color fought for the right to eat at public lunch counters, ride in the front of the bus, and attend the schools of their choice. Leaders like Dr. Martin Luther King brought people of all colors together in marches, sit-ins, and protests. Their battle was not with weapons and fists. Like Valentine, the civil rights workers followed the example of Jesus, fighting injustice with the power of love.

The Legend of the Valentine
Text Copyright © 2001 by Katherine Grace Bond
Illustrations Copyright © 2001 by Don Tate
Requests for information should be addressed to:

Zonderkidz™

The children's group of Zondervan

Grand Rapids, Michigan 49530
www.zonderkidz.com

ISBN 0-310-70039-6

All rights reserved. No part of this publication may be reproduced, stored in a retrieval system, or transmitted in any form or by any means–electronic, mechanical, photocopy, recording, or any other–except for brief quotations in printed reviews, without the prior permission of the publisher.

Printed in China
01 02 03 04 05 06 /v HK/ 10 9 8 7 6 5 4 3 2 1
Many thanks to Peggy King Anderson, Judy Bodmer, Janet Lee Carey, Roberta Kehle, Dawn Knight and Tammy Perron and to Le Roy Henderson of the African American History Museum, Chattanooga, Tennessee, for being an answer to prayer.